THIS WALKER BOOK BELONGS TO:

_____

_____

_____

First published 1993 by Walker Books Ltd
87 Vauxhall Walk, London SE11 5HJ

This edition published 2004

10 9 8 7 6 5 4 3 2 1

This book has been typeset
in Calligraphic 810 BT

Printed in China

British Library Cataloguing in
Publication Data: a catalogue record
for this book is available from
the British Library

ISBN 1-84428-488-3

www.walkerbooks.co.uk

For all at the
special care Baby Unit,
RMH, Belfast

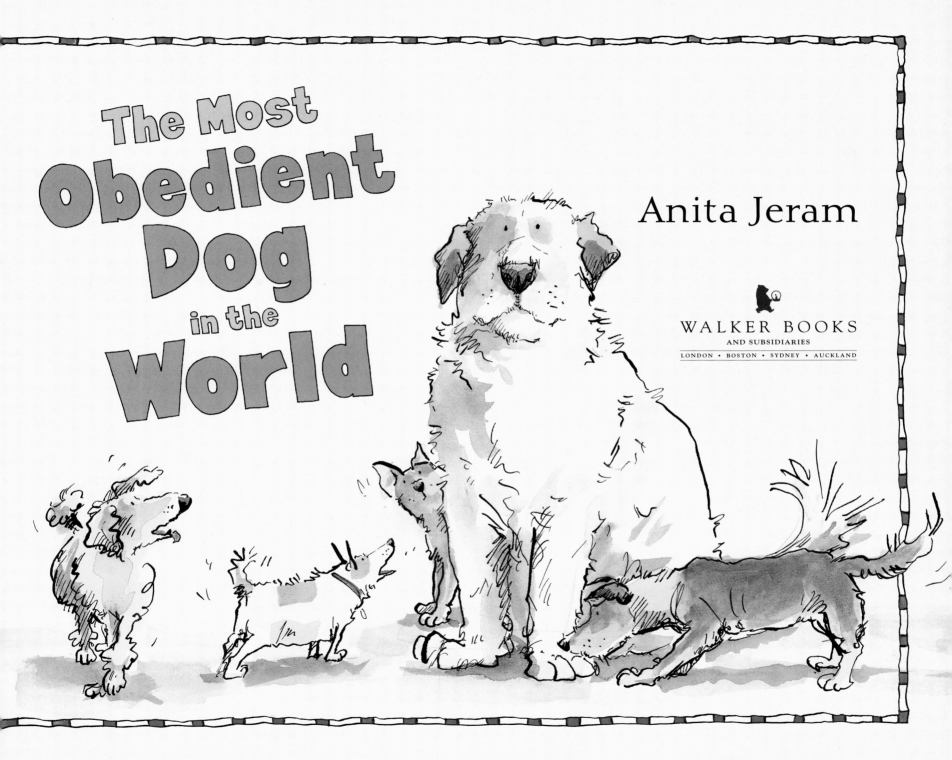

The Most Obedient Dog in the World

Anita Jeram

WALKER BOOKS
AND SUBSIDIARIES
LONDON · BOSTON · SYDNEY · AUCKLAND

The most obedient dog in the world was
waiting for something to happen,

when Harry came up the path.

"Hello, boy," said Harry.

The most obedient dog in the world wagged
his tail and started to follow Harry.

"No ... sit!" said Harry. "I won't be long."

And then he was gone.

"Why are you sitting there?"
asked a nosy bird.

"Are you going to sit
there all day?"

The most obedient dog in the world didn't answer.

He just sat and waited for Harry.

Big, fat raindrops began to fall.

"I'm off," said the bird. And he flew away.

Everyone ran for cover, except
the most obedient dog
in the world.

Thunder rumbled, lightning flashed
and then the hailstones fell...

Quite a lot of hailstones!

When the sun came out again
the bird flew back. The most
obedient dog in the world
was still sitting there
waiting for Harry.

"What a strange dog," people said as they passed.

Other dogs came
to have a look.
They sniffed and
nuzzled and nudged
and nipped,

but they soon got bored
and went away.

The most obedient dog in the world sat ...

and sat ... and sat ... and sat.

How long must he wait for Harry?

Just then, a cat came by.

"Quick!" said the bird, pulling his tail.
"Why don't you chase it?"

The dog's eyes
followed the cat.
His nose started
to twitch,

and his legs started to itch.
He couldn't sit still
any longer.

He sprang to his feet ...

and saw Harry!

"Good boy!" said Harry. "You waited!
Leave that cat. Let's go to the beach!"

The dog looked at the cat, and he looked at Harry.

Then he went to the beach with Harry.

After all, he was ...

the most obedient dog in the world!

WALKER BOOKS is the world's leading independent publisher of children's books. Working with the best authors and illustrators we create books for all ages, from babies to teenagers – books your child will grow up with and always remember. So…

FOR THE BEST CHILDREN'S BOOKS, LOOK FOR THE BEAR